FREDERICK WARNE
An Imprint of Penguin Random House LLC, New York

Published in 2021 by Frederick Warne,
an imprint of Penguin Random House LLC, New York.
Manufactured in China.

Visit us online at www.penguinrandomhouse.com.

ISBN: 9780241470138

PETER RABBIT™

I LOVE YOU, GRANDMA

Every DAY, I learn

something
NEW,

from
EACH
adventure

I *share* WITH YOU.

I'm **BRAVE** and STRONG

WHEN *you're* BY MY *side,*

and
being
MY
GUIDE.

THE *birds* SING A *tune*

as we
WALK,
hand
IN
hand,

OVER
the
HILLS

and
ACROSS
the
LAND.

As
I
grow
UP

AND
my
DREAMS
grow,
TOO,

the
WORLD
anew.

MY *secrets* SAFELY

you WILL *keep,*

As I
CLOSE
MY
eyes

AND *drift* OFF to SLEEP.

FOR
loving ME
LIKE
you
DO,

and
REMEMBER
I will
ALWAYS